SWAMP MONSTERS

by Mary Blount Christian
pictures by Marc Brown

SCHOLASTIC INC.
New York Toronto London Auckland Sydney

ISBN 0-590-93753-7

Text copyright © 1983 by Mary Blount Christian.
Illustrations copyright © 1983 by Marc Brown.
All rights reserved. Published by Scholastic Inc., 555 Broadway, New York, NY 10012, by arrangement with Puffin Books, a division of Penguin Books USA Inc.

12 11 10 9 8 7 6 5 4 3 2 1   6 7 8 9/9 0 1/0

Printed in the U.S.A.   24

First Scholastic printing, October 1996

For Jennifer Michelle Easter
M.B.C.

For Atha and Regina,
who let me draw people
M.B.

Crag pulled the tadpole by the tail.

It swam away behind some weeds.

"Stop teasing the tadpoles,"

Mrs. Swamp Monster said.

"And come eat your lunch."

Crag made a face.

"Snail stew,

kelp salad," he whined.

"Why can't we eat *good* things?"

"Yeah," Fenny said.

"Like ice cream

or pizza!"

He gave Spot a piece of snail.

7

Spot gobbled it up.

"Don't feed the 'gator at the table,"

Mrs. Monster said.

"It teaches him bad manners.

You know we swamp monsters

don't eat ice cream and pizza.

Those are *people* foods,

like in the books we read."

Crag pulled Spot's tail.

The 'gator let out a loud *gronk*!

"That's it!" Mrs. Monster said.
"Sometimes you both act
as bad as—as CHILDREN!
Go and play," she said.

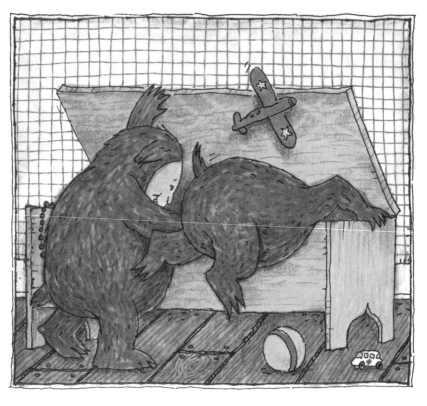

"Let's play Children," Crag said.

"Okay," Fenny said.

"That's a good game.

But we have to dress up first."

They dug through their toy boxes.

They found hats and
rubber boots to wear.
They found the people masks
they wore last Halloween.
They crawled out into the swamp.

11

"*RRRRRRRRroarrr*," Crag said.

"I am a child.

I am going to catch you!"

"Shh!" Fenny said.

"I hear noises over there."

They peeked through the bushes.

"What are *those*?" Crag asked.

"Don't touch that, Herbie!"

the tall one yelled.

"That's poison ivy!"

"Is that a people?" Crag asked.

"She looks like

the big one in our storybook,"

Fenny agreed.

"But I didn't think they were *real*!"

"Cindy, get back in line!

You'll get lost!

Jason, don't put rocks in your ears,"

the tall one yelled.

The tall one talked to herself.

"Oh, *why* did I take

Mrs. Smith's class today?

I hope she is well soon."

"Children!" she called.

"Get in line!

It's time to go!"

"Did you hear that?"

Crag asked Fenny.

"She called the short ones children."

Fenny nodded.

"I would like to see one

REAL close," he said.

They moved closer.

Suddenly the tall one grabbed them.

"You heard me!" she said.

"Get in line right now.

March!"

"Ms. Mumfrey," a girl whined.

"Tommy put a bug in my hair."

"Which one is Tommy?"

the tall one asked.

"She hit me," a boy said.

Ms. Mumfrey pulled them apart.

"But Mrs. Smith lets us
play like this," the boy said.

"Well, Mrs. Smith is sick.
You must be extra good for me."

"Listen," Crag said.

"She is not their real teacher."

"And she thinks we are with them."

"Let's go with them," Fenny said.

"We can see if the books are true."

Ms. Mumfrey marched them
to a big yellow bus.
Crag and Fenny got on the bus too.
The door shut.
The bus bumped and rumbled
down the road.

Soon the swamp was out of sight.
The bus stopped.

"Everyone out!" Ms. Mumfrey said.

The children punched and pushed

on the way out.

Crag and Fenny stumbled out too.

"Take off your coats," Ms. Mumfrey said.

"Look!" Fenny said.

"The children took off their skins.

They hung them up!"

"You too," Ms. Mumfrey told them.

She pulled and tugged at them.

"Your zippers must be stuck," she said.

The children sat at their desks.

"Take your seats,"

Ms. Mumfrey told Crag and Fenny.

Crag asked Fenny,

"Where should we take them?"

"I don't know," Fenny said.

"But we don't want to make her mad."

They picked up their chairs and
carried them toward the door.

The children laughed.

"I like the new kids," Tommy said.

"Stop that!" Ms. Mumfrey said.

"You would not do this to Mrs. Smith!"

27

She hit the desk with a ruler.

"Sit down in the seats," she said.

"It's time for our TV art lesson.

You there," she told Crag.

"Put on the TV."

Crag saw the box in the corner.

It was like the one in his storybook.

But he did not know how to put it on.

He didn't want her mad at him though.

He thought it might fit on his head.

So that is where he put it.

"Stop that!" Ms. Mumfrey yelled.

"The new kids are neat!"

Marshall said.

Ms. Mumfrey put the TV on the table.

She turned the knob.

A picture came on.

"Today we will finger-paint," it said.

Ms. Mumfrey smiled.

"Yes, we will finger-paint," she said.

The children got paints and paper.

Crag and Fenny found some too.

The children swooshed
paint on the paper.

"That looks like

paper painting to me," Crag said.

"But Ms. Mumfrey said to *finger*-paint."

"We don't want to make her mad,"

Fenny said.

They painted their fingers.

It felt good.

They took off their boots

and painted their toes.

The children giggled.

They all painted

their fingers and toes too.

Ms. Mumfrey held her head.

"Why me?" she moaned.

"It is lunchtime.

Come here if you need lunch money."

Crag and Fenny didn't

have anything like that.

They went to her desk.

Ms. Mumfrey put

a quarter, a dime, and a nickel

into Crag's hand.

"But I wanted ice cream,"

he told Fenny.

"Don't make her mad," Fenny said.

So Crag popped the money

into his mouth.

CRUNCH!
SCRUNCH!
SCRAWNCH!

Ms. Mumfrey gasped. Crag swallowed.

The money clinked into his tummy.

"Never do I want

another day like this!"

Ms. Mumfrey said.

She gave Crag more money.

"Don't eat this," she said.

"This is for the lunchroom."

The lunchroom was not to eat either.

That was where they lined up

to push and shove each other.

"Oh, boy!" Marshall said.

"Noodles and ice cream."

Crag and Fenny were glad

they could eat their storybook foods.

Crag looked at the noodles.

"They look like worms," he said.

"The ice cream looks

like snow," Fenny said.

"Maybe it tastes better

than it looks," Crag said.

"Take your seats," Ms. Mumfrey said.

"I mean, SIT DOWN!" she said.

Crag chased the noodles

all around his plate.

They wiggled away.

He stabbed some with his fork.

He got them almost to his mouth.

They flopped back to the plate.

Fenny tried to eat the ice cream.

It dripped all over him.

It felt sticky and cold.

"I wish I had snail stew," Fenny said.

After that they went outside.

"Now, go play," Ms. Mumfrey said.

"Look," Crag said.

"Those children hit

that big white berry with a stick.

And those are swinging

from a metal tree."

Then they saw it.

40

"It is like the swamp!" Crag said.

They both jumped into the fountain.

They splashed lovely

wet water on themselves.

The other children jumped in too.

"Eeeeek!" Ms. Mumfrey yelled.

"You act like—like MONSTERS!"

She wagged her finger at them.

"The principal

will straighten you out!"

"That would hurt," Crag said.

"I like being round," Fenny agreed.

They got out of the water.

Ms. Mumfrey dried them off.

They went inside.

"It is story time," she said.

"Put your heads on your desks."

Crag and Fenny were glad that

she didn't really mean it.

She only wanted them

to rest their heads on the desks.

"She sure talks funny," Crag said.

"Far, far away in a warm, wet swamp,"
Ms. Mumfrey read,
"lived some monsters."
Crag peeked at Fenny.
He looked sad too.
"They ate snails
and fish
and turtle eggs,"
she read.

43

Crag's tummy rumbled.

How he wished for some

good snail stew!

"Zzzzzzz," Ms. Mumfrey said.

She was asleep.

"Psst!" Fenny said.

"I want to go home."

"Me too," Crag said.

The two swamp monsters

tiptoed from the room.

They ran and ran and

they didn't stop

until they were home.

"I'm glad we saw children," Fenny said.

"And tried noodles and ice cream."

"But I'm glad to be home,"
Crag said.

"I like swamp life better,"
Fenny agreed.

Mrs. Monster was baking
mud pie for dessert.

"If we are real good,

do we get mud pie?"

Crag asked.

Mrs. Monster hugged them both.

"I don't see why not!

And if you are *extra* good,

I'll read a story too."

"Yeah," Crag said.

"A scary one!"

"About children!"

Fenny agreed.